Little Fairy's Christmas

The illustrations in this book were hand-crafted
using watercolour paints and ink.

First published in German as *Die kleine Elfe feiert Weihnachten* by
Verlag Urachhaus, Stuttgart in 2010. First published in English by
Floris Books, Edinburgh in 2010. This edition 2022. © 2010 Verlag
Freies Geistesleben & Urachhaus GmbH. English version © 2010,
2022 Floris Books. All rights reserved. No part of this publication
may be reproduced without prior permission of
Floris Books, Edinburgh www.florisbooks.co.uk
British Library CIP Data available. ISBN 978-178250-817-5
Printed in Poland through Hussar

FSC
www.fsc.org
MIX
Paper from
responsible sources
FSC® C167221

Floris Books supports sustainable
forest management by printing this
book on materials made from wood
that comes from responsible sources
and reclaimed material

Little Fairy's Christmas

Daniela Drescher

Floris Books

It was very, very cold. Snowflakes
danced through the air.

Faith, the little fairy, had become
lost in a snowstorm and blown far
away from home. She needed to find
somewhere warm to stay. Her wings
and toes were frozen stiff.

"Hello, little fairy," said a robin redbreast.
"What are you doing outside in this weather?"
"I'm lost and I need somewhere warm
to stay," said Faith.

"It will be warmer in the woods," said the kind robin. "Take this in case you get hungry on your journey." He gave her one of the last rosehips from the hedgerow.

"Thank you," said Faith, and she headed towards the trees.

"Hello, little fairy," said a
barn owl. "What are you doing
outside in the cold?"

"I'm lost and I need somewhere
warm to stay," said Faith.

The friendly owl flew through
the air and dropped a bag at the
fairy's bare feet. Inside she found lovely
thick socks and snug boots.

But before Faith could say thank you,
the owl had flown away.

It was getting late as Faith walked deeper into
the woods. The wind picked up and snow whirled
around her. Then she saw a little elf child hiding
in the roots of a tree.

"What are you doing out here in the snow?"
Faith asked.

"I was looking for Father Christmas, to show him the
way to our house," said the elf.
"But I lost my way in the
storm, and I'm cold and hungry."

"Here," said Faith, and she wrapped
the bag that the owl had given her
around the little elf.

Then she broke the rosehip in three:
one piece for the elf, one piece for herself,
and one piece for a raccoon, who looked
very hungry too.

Suddenly, deep in the forest, a light
glowed, becoming brighter and brighter.

As the light drew nearer,
Faith and the little elf child
gasped in surprise.
"It's Father Christmas!"
cried the elf excitedly.
"It's really him!"

"What are you two doing out here in this weather?" asked Father Christmas. "You should be tucked up in bed!"

"We're lost," said Faith. "Can you help us find somewhere warm to stay?"

Father Christmas let Faith and the little elf ride on his donkey. As they walked across the snowy white fields, the storm calmed. The moon shone brightly to show them the way.

When the sun came up, the elf shouted happily,
"There's my house!"

The little elf's family were so pleased he was
home safe. And amazed to see who else had come!

Father Christmas gave each grateful child
a present.

"Come inside!" said Mama elf to the visitors,
but Father Christmas had more parcels to deliver.

"Until next year!" he called.

The elf family welcomed Faith
into their little house.

"Snug and cosy at last!"
Faith said happily.

The elves asked Faith to stay
and they had a wonderful time
celebrating together.

And what present had
Father Christmas chosen for
Faith? A soft, blue hot-water
bottle to keep her nice and warm!

When the snow had finally melted,
Faith waved goodbye to her new
friends, and set off home.

Daniela Drescher is an internationally acclaimed author and illustrator. Born in 1966, she grew up in the suburbs of Munich, Germany. As a child, Daniela spent countless hours imagining castles in the hedgerows – homes for fairies and elves. She drew and painted until her pictures started to "come alive" and tell stories of their own.

Daniela was a children's painting and drawing therapist for ten years, using her own poetry in her therapeutic work.

Now the creator of more than forty children's books, Daniela still draws the fairies and elves she imagined as a child playing in the hedgerows.

"Fantasy is the key that we give to our children, so they can unlock and reshape the present."

Daniela Drescher

A selection of books by *Daniela Drescher*

Pippa and Pelle
in the Spring Garden
Daniela Drescher

Pippa and Pelle
in the Winter Snow
Daniela Drescher

Daniela Drescher
Pippa and Pelle
and the Birthday Gifts

Daniela Drescher
Norbert the Winter Gnome

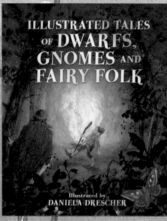

ILLUSTRATED TALES OF DWARFS, GNOMES AND FAIRY FOLK
Illustrated by
DANIELA DRESCHER

The Garden Adventures of Griswald the Gnome
Daniela Drescher

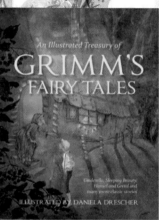

An Illustrated Treasury of
GRIMM'S FAIRY TALES
Cinderella, Sleeping Beauty, Hansel and Gretel and many more classic stories
ILLUSTRATED BY DANIELA DRESCHER

Daniela Drescher
In the Land of Fairies

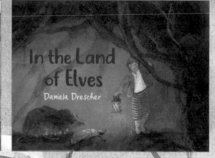

In the Land of Elves
Daniela Drescher

In the Land of Mermaids
Daniela Drescher

Daniela Drescher
Goodnight Sandman

Lily the Little Princess
Daniela Drescher

More adventures with
Faith, the little fairy

Little Fairy
Makes a Wish
Daniela Drescher

Little Fairy's
Meadow Party
Daniela
Drescher

Little Fairy
Can't Sleep
Daniela
Drescher